All by Himself?

written by
Elana K. Arnold

illustrated by
Giselle Potter

BEACH LANE BOOKS
New York   London   Toronto
Sydney   New Delhi

Because
years ago
before the child was even born
a farmer planted a seedling,

and because
after that
an arborist tended the tree
that grew from the seedling
the farmer had planted,

and because
last fall
a woodcutter felled the tree
that the arborist tended
that grew from the seedling
the farmer had planted,

and because
last spring
a woodworker carved
blocks from wood
that came from the tree
that the woodcutter felled
that the arborist tended
that grew from the seedling
the farmer had planted,

and because
last summer
an artist painted the blocks
that the woodworker carved
from the wood of the tree
that the woodcutter felled
that the arborist tended
that grew from the seedling
the farmer had planted,

and because
last month
a driver transported the blocks
that the artist painted
that the woodworker carved
from the wood of the tree
that the woodcutter felled
that the arborist tended
that grew from a seedling
the farmer had planted,

and because last week
a shopkeep displayed the blocks
that the driver transported
that the artist painted
that the woodworker carved

from the wood of the tree
that the woodcutter felled
that the arborist tended
that grew from a seedling
the farmer had planted,

and because
yesterday
the grandmother went to the shop
to buy the blocks
that the shopkeep displayed
that the driver transported
that the artist painted
that the woodworker carved
from the wood of the tree
that the woodcutter felled
that the arborist tended
that grew from a seedling
the farmer had planted...

because of all of this,
today
the child built a masterpiece.

All by himself!

And also . . .

with the grandmother

and the shopkeep

and the driver

and the artist

and the woodworker

and the woodcutter

and the arborist

and the farmer.

And of course . . .

the tree itself.

For anyone who has ever had help
building their dreams—that is to
say, for everyone
—E. K. A.

For Pia and Isabel
—G. P.

BEACH LANE BOOKS
An imprint of Simon & Schuster Children's Publishing Division
1230 Avenue of the Americas, New York, New York 10020
Text © 2022 by Elana K. Arnold
Illustration © 2022 by Giselle Potter
Book design by Lauren Rille and Lissi Erwin © 2022 by Simon & Schuster, Inc.
All rights reserved, including the right of reproduction in whole or in part in any form.
BEACH LANE BOOKS and colophon are trademarks of Simon & Schuster, Inc.
For information about special discounts for bulk purchases, please contact
Simon & Schuster Special Sales at 1-866-506-1949 or business@simonandschuster.com.
The Simon & Schuster Speakers Bureau can bring authors to your live event.
For more information or to book an event, contact the Simon & Schuster Speakers Bureau
at 1-866-248-3049 or visit our website at www.simonspeakers.com.
The text for this book was set in Archer Book.
The illustrations for this book were rendered in watercolor and ink.
Manufactured in China
0522 SCP
First Edition
10 9 8 7 6 5 4 3 2 1
Library of Congress Cataloging-in-Publication Data
Names: Arnold, Elana K., author. | Potter, Giselle, illustrator.
Title: All by himself / Elana K. Arnold ; illustrated by Giselle Potter.
Description: First edition. | New York : Beach Lane Books, [2022] | Audience: Ages 0–8. | Audience: Grades K–1. |
Summary: Illustrates that we are all connected and that no one goes through life—or builds anything—
all by themselves.
Identifiers: LCCN 2021047693 (print) | LCCN 2021047694 (ebook) | ISBN 9781534489899 (hardcover) | ISBN
9781534489905 (ebook)
Subjects: CYAC: Cooperation—Fiction.
Classification: LCC PZ7.A73517 Al 2022 (print) | LCC PZ7.A73517 (ebook) | DDC [E]—dc23
LC record available at https://lccn.loc.gov/2021047693
LC ebook record available at https://lccn.loc.gov/2021047694